Contents

*C = copper; B = bronze; S = silver; T = teacher; ( ) = the line must be played but cannot be assessed for a Medal; non-bold type = descant/soprano recorder; bold type = treble/alto recorder.

† and ‡ The lines at Copper level are in one of two pitch-groups, to reflect different approaches to note learning at this level.
† = group A and ‡ = group B. The choice of pitch-group has no bearing on the assessment.

group A(†)

group B(‡)

Just Teasing

Doris da Costa

AB 3134

One Sunny Morning

Brian Bonsor

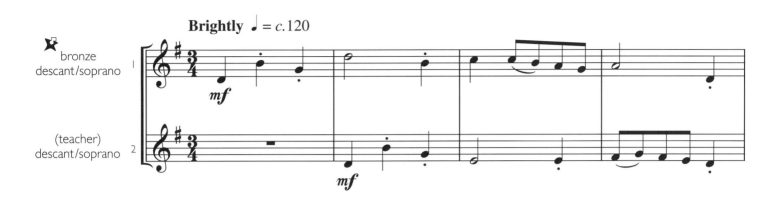

Up and Down the Stairs

Jane Sebba

AB 3134

The Chinese Dragon Dreams

Sally Adams

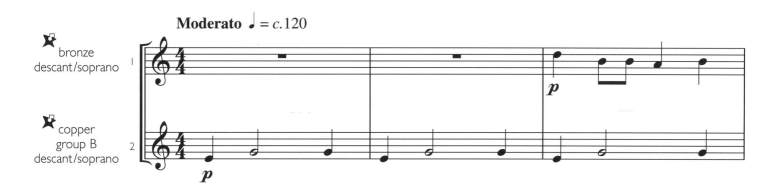

Lunar Seascape

Sally Adams

AB 3134

Golden Leaves

Andrew Challinger

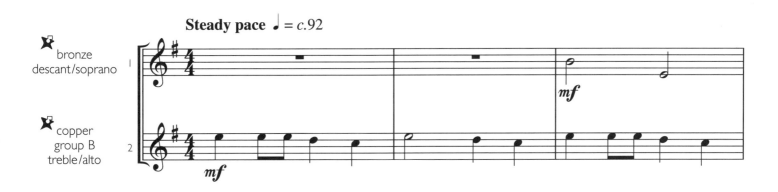

Butterflies

Doris da Costa

AB 3134

Just Thinking...

Brian Bonsor

Lazy Afternoon

Andrew Challinger

Trot to the Town on a Pinto Pony

Sally Adams

The Pendulum Swings

Brian Bonsor

AB 3134

Medieval Medley

David Gordon

Scotch Mist

Alan Bullard

AB 3134

Trotting Along

Brian Bonsor

Running for the Bus

Alan Bullard

AB 3134

Hoedown

Jonathan Leathwood

AB 3134

Copycats

Doris da Costa

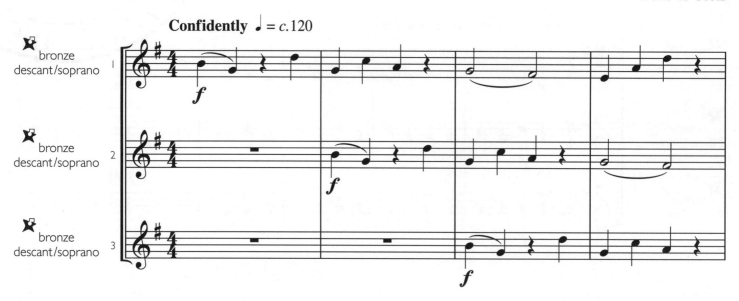

The Tyrolean Troll's Trip to Timbuktu

Sally Adams

AB 3134

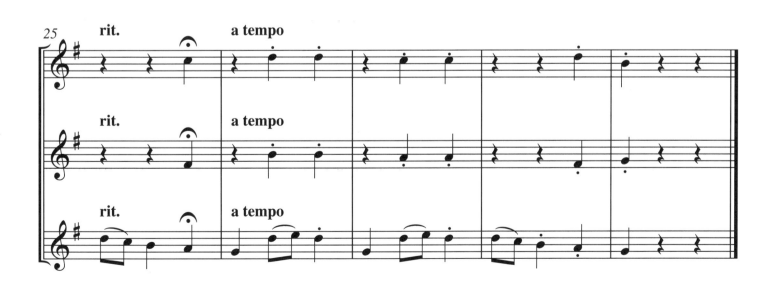

Green Flag

Sarah Watts

AB 3134

Gavotte

David Gordon

AB 3134